Touching Story Of 'Raphael, the Herald Angel'

A Texas grandmother has written a story likely to become a Christmas classic in the vein of "The Other Wise Men" or "The Littlest Angel." The new book is "Raphael, the Herald Angel."

The writer is Merle Minkert Hudson of Bryan. She is the aunt by marriage of Dale McCullough, son of Mrs. E. D. McCullough, 2213 Lipscomb. Mrs. Hudson, wife of Dan Hudson, a Bryan insurance agent, is the niece of the late W. S. McClung and Mrs. Maud McClain McClung of Amarillo and a cousin of the Rev. S. R. McClung, one-time pastor of a Baptist church in Amarillo.

Mrs. Hudson, who has been writing for The Houston Chronicle for the past five years, first created the story of Raphael to tell her grandchildren. She and Mr. Hudson have two children and four grandchildren.

The Raphael story now has been published by Channel Press of Great Neck, N.Y., and has been syndicated for newspaper use by The Hall Syndicate, Inc., of New York, N.Y.

Co-author of the book is newspaperman David Appel, feature editor of The Philadelphia Inquirer. Illustrator is Reisie Lonette, an artist of Long Island, N.Y., who found her three-year-old son an ideal model for her cherub sketches in "Raphael."

The sensitively illustrated 55-page book, six by nine inches in size, tells the story of a shy and modest angel named Raphael, choirmaster of heaven.

The warm-hearted story reveals how Raphael was chosen as herald angel to lead the celestial choirs to announce the arrival on earth of the most precious Gift ever bestowed, the Christ Child.

The story reports in tender fantasy the heavenly choirs' "good tiding of great joy." And then, the story tells of the disappointment of Raphael when ne finds that mankind does not welcome this Greatest of All Gifts.

Back in heaven, he resigns his choirmaster post and lives in seclusion meditating on what he considers to be his failure in announcing the arrival of the Christ Child.

Almost twenty centuries later, after his brooding on mankind's failure to rejoice at the nativity of the Christ Child and mankind's ill treatment of Jesus in His adult years, Raphael visits earth for a second time.

In this twentieth century visit lies the quiet joy of the little book, for Raphael finds mortals in churches on Christmas Eve commemorating the birth of Christ — and singing the same words the angels sang long ago.

And, appropriately enough, the rector of Trinity Church in New York has written to Mrs. Hudson for permission to use "Raphael" in Christmas Eve services this year.—**Patricia Masterman.**

RAPHAEL, THE HERALD ANGEL

RAPHAEL
THE HERALD ANGEL

By David Appel and Merle Hudson
Illustrated by Reisie Lonette

CHANNEL PRESS   GREAT NECK, NEW YORK

Library of Congress Catalog
Number 57–13472

To Elizabeth

"R aphael!"

In the rehearsal studio at the very end of the long corridor, three angel voices faded in the middle of a note, and three small pairs of angel wings fluttered. The cherubs had just heard the Great Voice summoning their singing teacher.

But the choirmaster continued to rap his baton in time to the interrupted melody. "Why have you stopped?" he asked. "Please,

please sing until I give you the signal. You'll never learn to be Heavenly singers if you don't obey the rules."

"*But . . .*" piped the first cherub.

"*. . . the Great Voice . . .*" trilled the second.

"*. . . . . . just called you!*" warbled the third.

"Nonsense," Raphael said. "Why would the Great Voice call me? The Great Voice has *never* called my name, and I have been here for eons. You cherubs are always thinking of some clever way to get out of choir practice!" And again the choirmaster rapped his baton.

"Raphael!"

Now four pairs of angel wings fluttered. Now four voices halted abruptly. This, then, was no cherubic prank—they *had* heard the Great Voice, filling the rehearsal studio with sweet tones. "That's my name!" gasped Raphael. "I must leave," he said as he stepped over the stacks of music piled on the floor of the room. "You stay right here," he instructed as he squeezed between the musical instruments cluttering the entrance. "And please," he entreated as he rushed out the door, "please try to be little angels!"

Flying down the long corridor toward the Majestic Portals, Raphael asked himself question after question: "Why am I wanted? Why would a choirmaster be summoned to the Mighty Place? What can have happened?"

At the entrance he hesitated, arranging his robes to hide a few unfortunate inkstains. In his haste he had carried several sheets of music with him. Now holding them behind his back, Raphael shyly crossed into the brilliant light of the Mighty Place.

The room was full. They were all here—the messengers, darting through the air on silver wings; the elders, sitting close in quiet deliberation; the scribes, busy with their writing instruments. Even the archangels Michael and Gabriel were in the room. And all of them, Raphael thought ruefully, seemed to know exactly what was going on, and just what to do—all of them, that is, except him.

Then, just as the choirmaster nervously shifted the few pages of music from one hand to another, all activity stopped. Not even the rustle of an angel's wing could be heard.

8

And the Great Voice spoke: "Let us open the Book."

One of the scribes rose, holding high the golden volume in which he had been writing.

"Read my Promise," commanded the Voice.

The angel turned the pages of the tome, and ran his finger down one of the sheets until he came to the proper passage. Then, slowly and tenderly, he read. "The Promise is this: 'The people of earth, the people that walk in darkness, shall see a great light. Unto them a son shall be given . . . and his name shall be called Wonderful, Counsellor, the mighty God, the everlasting Father, the Prince of Peace.'"

"My children," said the Great Voice, "the time to fulfill this Promise is at hand."

"Amen," whispered Raphael, along with the rest of the Heavenly Assembly.

Again the Great Voice spoke: "Our beloved Gabriel has just returned from earth. Now it is fitting that my Holy Gift be announced to *all* the peoples of the world. My children, one of you shall go forth to make our great news known."

What an honor! Angel voices rippled, tinkled, buzzed, murmured, and hummed in excitement. Who would be chosen?

"Who but a messenger?" thought Raphael. "Many of them have been to earth. They know the way." Turning to a neighbor, the choirmaster whispered his prediction.

"I don't agree," the angel said. "A scribe will be chosen. We scribes have kept the Record, and know all that has ever happened."

Raphael shook his head. "We are both wrong. How silly of us! Gabriel will be sent to earth again. He will sound his golden trumpet to announce the Holy Gift. And if it isn't Gabriel, it will be Michael. Yes, I am sure of that—an archangel will be God's envoy!"

Raphael glanced about in satisfaction, his mind at rest. But even as he did so, his expression changed.

"Yet if an archangel is to be selected, why have *I* been summoned to the Mighty Place?" For an instant he considered the question, and then a happy smile lighted his face. "Now I know—the message will be delivered in song! And Lemuel, the leading tenor in my own

9

Hallelujah Choir, will sing it! That is why our Father has summoned me—so that I may be present when this wonderful honor is accorded my dearest friend!"

Indeed, Lemuel was known to possess the most expressive, the most lyrical singing voice in Heaven. But not only for this did Raphael admire him; apart from their close association in the choir, they were inseparable friends.

It was, in fact, amusing to watch the two angels walking side by side in the streets of the Beautiful City, deep in conversation. Raphael was better able to express himself in music than in words;

as he walked his hands seemed to search the air, as if there he might find the right phrase or sentence. His robes flowed and billowed with each long stride. His tall figure seemed ever to be rushing forward. Lemuel, however, was short and round, like so many tenors. Hurrying along, skipping on every third or fourth step so that he might keep pace with the choirmaster, he nevertheless noticed all that went on around him. He might pause to straighten a cherub's halo, or to welcome a newcomer with a smile, and yet would never miss one word of conversation.

"So it will be Lemuel," thought Raphael. "My, my, how we will have to rehearse! We shall have to change our whole schedule of classes immediately!"

And in his mind, the choirmaster began to make plans. He'd hold choir practice earlier, and shift the cherubim classes to late afternoon. . . .

But even as Raphael was thinking, a sudden change came over him. It was as if one, then ten, then a hundred, and then a thousand sunbeams were shining on him. It was as if a multitude of organs were thundering magnificent chords of music. And he seemed alone, completely alone. In wonder, he waited.

"Raphael!" the Great Voice commanded. *"Raphael, step forward."*

Had he really heard his name called again? The sheets of music slipped from the choirmaster's fingers, and fluttered to the floor. He moved as in a dream. All eyes, he sensed, were on him.

Humbly, very humbly, he moved to the front of the room. Quietly, very quietly, other angels stepped aside to let him pass. With each slow step, the pitch pipe dangling from a ribbon across his chest swayed. Raphael's eyes were wide, his head raised high.

Perfect silence again came over the room, and then the Great Voice spoke:

"Raphael, let there be proper music on this occasion. Let there be songs of exultation and joy. Let the angelic voices ring out. Choose well, choirmaster, from among your singers. Train them in songs of gladness and of great tidings. Let their anthems proclaim my Gift, and the fulfillment of my Promise to mankind."

Raphael trembled. This was too much to comprehend. He wanted to cry out, to shout his fears: "Not me—I am only a choirmaster. I am just a musician. I have never been to earth. I have never even been out of the Beautiful City."

But there was no need to speak. His thoughts had already been fathomed.

"True, Raphael," the Great Voice said. "You have never sung on earth, nor escorted a choir to that place. But never before has there been such an occasion. Now mankind is to receive the most precious Gift I can bestow. Nothing less than a choir of angels can serve to announce the news. Raphael, you will herald the event. *You* will be my Herald Angel!"

"I cannot believe it," the choirmaster thought. "I just cannot believe it." He struggled to find words that would eloquently describe his emotions. "Never before . . ." Raphael started to say, but his vision fogged and his thoughts were blurred.

"Never before have angels . . ." he began again, slowly turning to leave. But his voice choked with wonderment; he looked wordlessly at each of the angels in the chamber; and then, joy and astonishment in every word, he whispered at last:

"Never before have angels sung for mortals!"

As the Herald Angel approached the Portals, Michael stepped aside. Outside the Mighty Place, Gabriel waited, his trumpet tucked under his arm; and he too acknowledged with a graceful bow the honor given to Raphael. Messengers paused respectfully; the elders spoke words of encouragement.

But the choirmaster heard none of it, noticed nothing. With head bent slightly forward, he mumbled the same phrase over and over as he walked and then rushed and then flew down the long corridors toward his studio. *"Never before . . . never before . . . never before have angels sung for mortals!"*

Alone in the studio where rehearsals were held every afternoon, Raphael paced restlessly from one end of the room to the other. At the organ he paused, pressed down one key, still another, a third, and then shook his head. He wandered to a corner where the great harp was standing; he stroked the strings, bringing forth a fragment of a song. But again the Herald Angel was displeased.

No, he decided, the choirs could not use any of the old hymns they knew so well to announce the Gift. There must be new music, great music, for the Great Event. And to write it would require the assistance of his entire staff.

Later that day, messengers winged their way through the Beautiful City, asking each of the leading musicians, composers, arrangers and lyricists to attend a special meeting. In the studio, meanwhile, apprentices prepared for the conference. From the shelves they carried huge volumes containing the words and notes of all the songs that had ever been heard in Heaven. At a table they put sheaves of paper, ruled for musical notation, with ink and quills arranged neatly alongside.

At the appointed hour, Raphael's staff gathered around the table. Each, of course, had a different answer to the question of why the special meeting had been arranged. And so great was their excitement that the confusion only increased as they guessed and speculated. One angel whispered to his neighbor, "Raphael, I hear, is going to visit the world." But by the time the message had been repeated all around the conference table, it somehow became "Raphael's hair is growing too visibly curled."

Thus when the Herald Angel arrived, the musicians waited expectantly. Now, at last, they would learn the truth.

Raphael bustled to his place at the table, glanced briskly about the room, and said, "Good, good! You are all here. That's fine. Splendid. There's no time to lose. We must start today, this very minute. Yes, this very minute."

"Start what, Raphael?" asked an arranger.

"What? Oh yes, of course. I will explain it very quickly, my friends, because we have important work ahead of us. Therefore it is urgent that we get started immediately."

"Started at what, Raphael?" asked a harpist.

"At what? At what, you ask! Only the most important mission ever assigned to a group of angelic musicians! A great honor has been given us, and we must waste no time fulfilling it. The time is short. *We must get to work!*"

"At WHAT, Raphael?" shouted all the arrangers, composers, singers, lyricists and musicians.

The Herald Angel's voice was low, barely a whisper. "We must create the most beautiful music ever heard. And then . . ."

"And then?" echoed the angels.

"A Heavenly Choir will sing our music for man!"

"*For man!*" they chorused. "Why?" "How?" "When?"

"My dear colleagues, if you will just stop asking me so many things at once, I shall explain. We have the very best of reasons. Our Father is about to give a Gift, a very precious Gift, to mankind. And we—we are to herald the event in song!

"That is why I have called you here today," he continued. "We must work together, work as we have never worked before, to create music so beautiful, so perfect that man will understand the joy and wonder of God's Gift. My friends, all of you must give your utmost!"

The Herald Angel looked hopefully about the table, waiting for suggestions. Several of his colleagues rearranged the papers placed before them on the table; a few peered out the window; one studied the tip of his pen; another carefully smoothed his wings; but no one replied. Finally a lyricist broke the long silence. "I'm sure we'd all know what to do if we were singing here in the Beautiful City for angels, Raphael. But none of us has ever been to earth. Not one of us has ever sung for men. We don't know where to begin."

At the end of the table, Lemuel coughed politely for attention.

"Fortunately," he said, "Raphael anticipated that problem. As a matter of fact, I've been conferring with many of the angels who have visited earth in the past. Shall I read my notes, Raphael?"

And then, almost before the Herald Angel could nod in agreement, the tenor unfurled a scroll, cleared his throat, and began:

"The problem is that the men and women of the world rarely recognize us as angels when they see us. Somehow we must convince them that we are indeed Heaven-sent, and have news of supreme importance to bring them. I've been told that on earth, when leaders wish to announce a significant event, they send trumpeters through the streets, and messengers proclaim the occurrence from turrets

and from house-tops. We must do something similar, I feel, to win mankind's confidence and attention."

Now a clamor arose from Raphael's staff:

"Perhaps three great claps of thunder to begin . . ."

"A brilliant flash of heavenly fire . . ."

"Trumpet blasts . . ."

"Wait, wait!" Raphael cried. "You go too fast. Let me tell you what is to happen that night. Let us try to visualize the scene together. Immediately the Gift is made, we must announce it."

Raphael's eyes shone as he spoke. "Just imagine—at first only a few people in the streets will hear our song. But they will stop to listen. Some will shout for joy. Perhaps others will pound on the doors of the nearby houses . . ."

The angels at the table, caught up by Raphael's vision, forgot their manners. One after another, they interrupted.

"Some will be in the midst of their labors," said a lyricist. "They will put down their tools, and listen."

"Others will be sleeping," added the First Harpist, "but they will be aroused by the great choir in the Heavens."

"Servants will call upon masters, and masters will call upon servants to come to hear," declared the Assistant Arranger.

"Kings, rich men, poor men, everyone everywhere will be swept up by this music—Heavenly music, heard on earth for the first time," shouted Lemuel.

"But," a composer suddenly cautioned them, "some may panic. There will be screams of fear."

"Yes," his neighbor said, "you are right. They will run and hide."

The angels at the table stopped in discouragement and confusion, and looked to Raphael.

"Fear," the Herald Angel said, "can make men deaf. Fear can close their eyes. And so we must explain why mortals need not be frightened. Let us immediately proclaim the words, 'Fear not.' Perhaps we'll even repeat them. Let us make it so clear that even those who are in terror will understand that ours is a message of good tidings and great joy."

The writers set to work, conferring, comparing, selecting. The composers fitted words to notes. And Raphael was everywhere, rushing from keyboard to writing desk, humming, revising, suggesting, helping, correcting. His fingers were stained with ink, but pride gleamed from his face, for he knew their songs would be masterpieces. The hymns soared as they told of God's glory; their sweet low tunes pictured His strength and His love; notes of clarion beauty described His compassion.

Now came the problem of picking just the right voices to sing this magnificent music.

"Lemuel," the Herald Angel said, "we will make a tour of Heaven, you and I, and we'll select the very best singers in the Beautiful City. We'll start with every angel in our own Hallelujah Choir, of course. But with the other singing groups we must be very careful and most selective. We cannot use one more singer than we need, and we must not include one voice that isn't perfect."

Together the two friends walked to the part of the Heavenly Fields where the evening begins. It was time for angels to fly to the stars and light them for the night; time for the Vesper Chorus to sing. In the purple and violet shadows, Raphael and Lemuel listened; and as the last lustrous song ended, the Herald Angel turned to his companion.

"Lemuel, we must use the Vesper singers."

"Which of them?" asked the tenor.

"All of them."

"*All* of them?"

"Yes. But remember, Lemuel, that our chorus cannot become too large; and so from now on let us pick and choose with great care."

They went next to hear the Jubilee Chorus, taking care to stand safely back in a cushion of clouds where they would not be jolted and jarred, dazzled and deafened by the blasts of trumpets and thunder which always accompanied this choir's songs. But even in the distance, Raphael found that he couldn't stop the tap-tap-tap of his feet as he listened to the exultant hymns the chorus sang.

"How terrible," Raphael said. "How wonderful!"

"What do you mean? What's terrible? What's wonderful?"

"Such wonderful music," replied the Herald Angel. "But isn't it

terrible—we shall have to use every one of the Jubilee singers! Our
Heavenly Choir is growing so vast that I'll never be able to rehearse
them all properly."

It was quite the same when the two angels winged their way to
the part of the Beautiful City where the morning begins, there to
listen to the music of the Angelus Chorus, sounding like a garden
of silver bells heard across a vast expanse of white clouds. Which,
which, which to choose? Lemuel saw the concern on Raphael's face.

"Perhaps," he suggested with a gentle smile, "perhaps we should
use all of them."

"That's it," shouted Raphael. "All of them!"

But as the two angels approached the Rainbow Field where the
Cherubim Choir could be heard, the choirmaster suddenly stopped.
"Lemuel," he declared, "we must now be firm. We must be strong.

You and I know there are no voices more beautiful than those of the cherubim. But just think what will happen at rehearsals . . ."

"They'll tug at each other's wings," said Lemuel.

"And go sliding down sunbeams."

"They'll fling stardust all over us, and play hide-and-seek in the clouds."

"We must be very careful," insisted the Herald Angel.

"I agree."

Raphael and Lemuel listened with stubborn expressions on their faces as the cherubim began their hymn of abiding love. "Such innocence in their voices," whispered the tenor. "Don't let yourself be carried away," the Herald Angel warned him.

Now the cherubim floated and fluttered to a cloud, and from on high their pure voices trilled and chimed an anthem of adoration.

"Such enchanting tenderness," admitted the choirmaster. "Don't weaken," reminded Lemuel.

At the conclusion of the performance, the Herald Angel turned to his companion:

"Lemuel, I want to ask you a purely technical question. A musical question. Do you agree that it would be effective musicianship to include at least one cherubic voice in the Heavenly Choir on the night the Gift is given?"

"Most certainly, Raphael—but just one."

"Of course, we'd have to chance that during rehearsals he'd pour a bucket of dew into the tuba, or push a cloud between the choirs and the conductor."

"You can almost count on it, Raphael. One or a dozen—where there are cherubim, there's bound to be mischief."

"One or a dozen—hmmmmmm." The Herald Angel considered the question. "It would be folly," he finally declared.

"Pure folly!"

The two friends looked at each other. They were firm in their decision. They turned to leave the Rainbow Field. But there was just one thing they had to tell the cherubim first.

"At rehearsal tomorrow," said Raphael, "we want to see all of you."

Then he turned again to his companion. "On the night the Child is born, Lemuel, Heaven will be emptied of all its singers. The people of earth will hear the most glorious music of all time. And the Event, dear friend, demands just that!"

It is one thing to be a musician, and another to deliver a speech before all the choirs of Heaven. On the night before the first rehearsal, Raphael sat alone in his office, his fingers drumming nervously on his desk. Scraps of paper littered the floor; on each of them he had tried unsuccessfully to outline the talk he knew he must make the following morning.

It was urgent, he felt, that each of the angel singers understand the deep importance of the mission assigned by the Heavenly

27

Father. Raphael wondered whether he should ask Michael to deliver the speech for him. Or perhaps one of the elders.

But no—this was his responsibility. And so far into the night, Raphael wrote his speech, and then rehearsed it just outside the Gates, where there were only clouds and stars to hear him.

The next morning, tired but confident, Raphael walked toward the field where the choirs were to meet. He had gone only part of the way, however, when he came upon the three cherubs who attended his Echo Choir class.

"Good morning, Herald Angel!" piped the first cherub.

"May we help you carry your papers . . ?" trilled the second.

". . . and your baton?" warbled the third.

"Thank you, children," the choirmaster said. "That is very kind of you. Very thoughtful."

Gratefully, Raphael turned his possessions over to the cherubs, proceeded to the field, and mounted the gentle slope from which he would address the singers of Heaven. Assembled before him, eager and aglow, were the five angelic choirs. All bowed their heads in prayer, their golden halos and golden wings gleaming in the sun.

Raphael looked up a moment later. "My notes, please," he whispered to the three cherubs.

"We were playing in a cloud . . ." piped the first.

". . . and put them down just for an instant . . ." trilled the second.

". . . but the cloud has blown away!" warbled the third.

No notes! How then could the choirmaster find words for all that he had hoped to explain? How could he describe the Promise made when God created the world? Or tell how wonderful yet how complex a creature is man, how sometimes he does not know what is best for him?

Well, thought Raphael, *I can only try!*

"All of us," he began, "are our Father's children. Here in Heaven, there is not a moment when we are not surrounded by His love."

Raphael's voice faltered, but in the field the choirs listened with reverent expectancy.

"We angels of the Beautiful City know that His love has no

bounds. On earth, however, there are many men and women, and even little children, who are not aware of our Father's sweet compassion."

Raphael stood straight, his robes flowing in long lines.

"Fellow angels—our Father is about to give His beloved Son as a Gift to man, so that they may *all* come to know the wonder of His way. And you and I have been entrusted to deliver this wondrous message to the world. We have been chosen to proclaim the birth of a prince, the Prince of Peace, from the Heavens. And because of our message, because of the songs we shall sing, mankind will come to know, accept and love God's Offering."

"How glorious!" chorused the angels. "How blessed we are!"

"Well then," said Raphael with all the briskness he could muster, "let us begin our rehearsal. To your places, everyone! Jubilee Chorus, stay right where you are. Hallelujah singers, I want you farther to my right. Angelus—a little closer, please. Vesper singers— back and to the left, if you will. Now cherubim—will you be kind enough to hand out the music? It's all marked for each choir. And then hurry back to your places. No mischief on the way, either!"

In a few moments the choirs were in their places. The Herald Angel raised both hands, calling for the rapt attention of the singers. Alert, anxious to perform correctly, they waited. Lemuel, the tenor soloist, stepped forward. "Fear not," he sang . . .

Fear not, fear not! for behold
I bring you good tidings . . .

Lemuel's bell tones lingered in the air. Then Raphael brought his arms down in a sweeping gesture, a mighty signal to begin.

No angel in Heaven is likely ever to forget that moment. Messengers hovered, transfixed in the air. Scribes dropped their pens in astonishment. Elders looked about in amazement. And Raphael clapped his hands to his ears.

It was awful! The Hallelujah Choir was singing music so high and shrill that their voices broke in squeaks and squeals. The Angelus Chorus rumbled, grumbled and growled. The Vesper singers couldn't even stay in unison, each one struggling lamely to adjust

to the unfamiliar key and style of the music that had been placed before him. The cherubim . . .

Suddenly, each voice faded; and each head automatically turned toward the front row, where the Cherubim Choir sat, quiet as clouds on a windless morning, looks of pure innocence on every cherubic face, every cherubic eye fixed steadily on the choirmaster, dutifully awaiting his instructions.

Raphael spoke with a patience he did not at that moment feel. "In the future," he quietly announced, "we will relieve the cherubim of the responsibility of distributing the music!"

When at last each choir had received its proper pages, the Herald Angel again raised his arms high, and at his command the multitude of Heavenly voices burst forth:

Glory, glory to God in the highest!

This time it was even more beautiful than Raphael had expected. The ringing notes filled the Heavenly City, and now angels feasted on the wondrous music. One anthem led into another; the music rose in crescendo to the peak where Raphael knew the message should be announced:

Peace, on earth peace, good will to men!

The hymn was sung and the rehearsal was over; and Raphael could scarcely find a fault. There had been a few passages which could have glowed a bit more, but he knew that all would be perfect with only a little practice. After all, this was the first time the choirs had sung together.

Only Lemuel was not pleased. "Raphael," he said, "I must have a word with you."

"Yes, Lemuel?"

"The music was beautiful."

"I am glad."

"But you have paid so much attention to the music, Raphael, that you haven't thought how we will look to the people on earth."

"We'll look like angels, of course," the choirmaster replied.

"No, no!" the tenor said impatiently. "That's not what I mean. Try to remember how pretty a sight it is to see the cherubim perform on a golden morning. Each beautiful little angel is circled in a halo of sunlight. Or watch the Vesper Choir, silhouetted against the violet hues of the sky at sundown. Raphael, we must be sure that the Heavenly singers are not only marvelous to hear, but glorious to see."

"Lemuel," the Herald Angel declared, "I don't know how I'd manage without you! What a splendid idea."

Back in the Beautiful City, the two angels learned that the skies were indeed going to be at their most magnificent on the night the

Gift was given. The constellations would glimmer and gleam. The winds would be at their softest. And one star of burning beauty would shine and shimmer high above a little town on earth named Bethlehem.

"The darkness itself shall be comforting. Clouds will gather like silver draperies across the sky. And we singers," Lemuel exulted, "will take our places behind those clouds."

"Can't you see how beautiful it will be?" cried Raphael. "The moment the Child is born, you, Lemuel, will walk through the clouds alone. Rays of silver and white from this glorious star of wonder will shine upon you. You will sing slowly, my friend, and lovingly, comfortingly, soothingly. 'Fear not'—and then you'll pause —'Fear not.' Sing the entire passage twice, to give mankind time to assemble, to look up to the Heavens and listen. Then the winds, soft and steady, will draw back the curtain of clouds—and behold! the Heavenly Choir will be revealed, singing in splendor!"

Raphael paused, and smiled quietly at his friend. "You have given me one more idea. But I cannot discuss it yet."

The second rehearsal was thoroughly satisfactory—except, of course, for one interruption. All had gone well until the Jubilee Chorus rose to sing; indeed, the day remained peaceful until the trumpet accompaniment began. Then at once it became painfully obvious that somehow the cherubim, even under the watchful eyes of the angel choirs, had stuffed stardust into the golden horns. Dust sprayed here and there; singers sputtered, coughed, sneezed and wheezed. Stardust landed on eyebrows, flickered on eyelashes, glinted from wings, and covered the pages of music.

When order was restored, Raphael asked the angel choirs to repeat the portion of their hymn which began with the words, "Glory to God in the Highest." It was plain from the way he spoke that he was not displeased, but was simply considering some innovation. Thereafter, at each of the rehearsals, the singers were instructed to repeat this phrase.

Several of the more observant angels noticed that whenever they sang these six beautiful words a second time, Raphael would slowly turn sideways. Only his left side now faced the Heavenly Choir, yet he still directed the singers as enthusiastically as ever with both hands.

"Puzzling, isn't it?" asked an alto.

"I've never seen a conductor do such a thing before," replied a harpist.

"Did you notice," asked a bass, "that this sideways gesture always comes promptly at the end of the closing passage? I wonder what is in his mind when he does that."

What the angel chorus did not yet know was that their director was preparing for a moment he was sure would arrive. In his imagination, Raphael could picture great multitudes looking up from earth as the clouds drew aside. He could see their faces shine with joy and trust as they heard Lemuel reveal the coming of the Son. He visualized the rapture with which they would fall to their knees to thank God for His precious Gift. And as their hearts opened, the Herald Angel believed, men would want to join with the angels in singing "Glory to God in the Highest."

Raphael would be ready! During the closing passage, he would turn toward earth . . .

With one arm he would lead the Hallelujah Choir, the Vesper Chorus, the Jubilee singers, the Angelus Choir and the Cherubim Choir . . .

With the other, he would lead all mankind as they blended their voices with the angels in song.

What a finale it would make for this momentous event! What a miracle of love it would be! How pleased the Lord would be with all His children!

But this was Raphael's secret. He held it close and told no one.

Even a newcomer to the Beautiful City would have realized that this was a special day.

Wherever they went, whatever they did, the angels of Heaven could think of nothing and speak of nothing but the Gift that was to be given to man that night.

"Tonight," they murmured to each other, "the Child will be born."

Wherever they went, whatever they did, they uttered prayers of gratitude.

"Tonight," they said to each other in hushed tones, "mankind will come to see how dearly God loves the world."

In the large hall at the very end of the corridor, the Heavenly Choir had just completed the last rehearsal. This time the performance was perfect in every detail; not even the cherubim were prompted to mar its absolute beauty.

Now all that remained was to wait.

The moments passed. Messengers were poised to soar into the air from one corner of Heaven to the next to announce that the Great Event was taking place. The scribes sat with their books open, their pens ready.

"Lemuel, Lemuel," whispered Raphael as he nervously knotted and twisted the ribbon from which his pitch pipe dangled, "have I forgotten anything? Will it be all right? Are we prepared?"

"It will be magnificent, my friend," the tenor assured him.

"Oh, Lemuel, I pray that you are right."

The musicians tuned their instruments. Clouds floated gently in the sky. The Star of Bethlehem rose high in the Heavens.

And on earth, it was the time when all the men and women had been ordered to their cities to be taxed.

And all went to be taxed, every one into his own city.

And Joseph also went up from Galilee, out of the city of Nazareth, into Judaea, unto the city of David, which is called Bethlehem; because he was of the house and lineage of David:

To be taxed with Mary his espoused wife, being great with child. And so it was, that, while they were there, the days were accomplished . . .

A Child was born in a manger.

Above, at that very instant, behind the silver curtain of clouds, silently, with scarcely a rustle of their wings and robes, the Heavenly choirs were assembling. From the Gates of the Beautiful City, down starlit paths, they streamed to their appointed places.

Raphael, the Herald Angel, stood before his singers, ready to give them the long-rehearsed, long-awaited signal. The choirs watched their leader breathlessly.

Raphael closed his eyes in silent prayer and thanksgiving. Then slowly he raised his arms—high, high, higher. This was the moment! The air was charged with expectancy. No night had ever been so still, yet so softly alive.

Down, down swept the Herald Angel's arms!

Lemuel, whose voice was the most beautiful in all Heaven, walked slowly through the silver clouds, brilliant white beams from one bright star illuminating his way. His voice filled the universe as he smiled gently, tenderly down at earth:

> *Fear not, fear not! for behold*
> *I bring you good tidings of great joy,*
> *Which shall be to all people.*

Now Lemuel moved closer to earth, repeating his message; and again his rich tones reached to the earth and stars:

> *For unto you is born this day*
> *In the city of David a Saviour,*
> *Which is Christ the Lord.*
> *And this shall be a sign unto you;*
> *Ye shall find the Babe wrapped*
> *In swaddling clothes—lying in a manger!*

Lemuel sang the passage comfortingly, lovingly, proudly; and as he concluded Raphael felt upon his cheek the soft wind that had come to draw back the cloud curtain.

Down swept the choirmaster's hand for the signal to all the choirs to unite their voices. Jubilant praise burst in a celestial cascade from the Heavenly singers.

How the music and the words reached into one's spirit! How the great choir matched the great occasion! With what feeling did they

magnify the Lord! With what range and volume did their voices echo among the stars!

"Never, never before have angels sung for mortals," thought the Herald Angel. Now, for the very first time, it was happening. Surely, felt Raphael, no one could resist this revelation, the splendor of this night, or the power of this mighty sound.

Even at this moment, he knew, the people on earth would be yearning to shout their praises and to sing of their adoration. And he would give them the signal which would invite them to join in the Heavenly hymn!

The choir was approaching those final lines, that place where the Herald Angel would carry out his plan. Heaven and earth, in song together! Angels and man, as one great voice. Just one more instant!

And then the choirs were triumphantly singing the majestic words, "Glory to God in the Highest."

Slowly the Herald Angel turned toward earth. With his left hand he led the Hallelujah Choir, the Angelus, the Jubilee singers, the Vesper Chorus and the cherubim.

With his right hand he would give the signal to mankind. NOW! he cried aloud, and his arm descended! *NOW!*

But from the earth . . . there came no sound.

No wave of human voices, no sea of hallelujahs, no mighty hymn. Nothing except the half cry of a new born child.

The Heavenly Choir had finished its hymn; Raphael looked earthward in astonishment. No throng was gazing unto Heaven—only a few shepherds in a field, who seemed sore afraid. Above, the star was bright; from the manger there radiated a glorious light. But elsewhere there was only darkness. Raphael's gaze swept the Judaean landscape. There were no throngs moving worshipfully toward Bethlehem. He turned to the distance, and could see no multitude coming over the hills. He turned to search the streets of the little town, but again he heard only the cry of a child.

"It is impossible," thought the Herald Angel, "that we have been singing, and that none but a few shepherds heard us. Impossible!"

Yet the hills and the streets were dark and empty and quiet. There was no evidence that mankind was aware of the beauty and the wonder of this night; even the shepherds on the hillside were yet silent and still, only confused by the signs above.

Sorrow such as he had never known before filled Raphael. "I have failed," he said. "I have failed."

Somehow, somewhere, he had made a grievous error. Perhaps he had frightened mankind. Perhaps he had not chosen the proper words, the music which would help the people of earth to understand the Heavenly message.

The fault, he decided as he looked down into the indifferent darkness and silence of the earth, was his. Because he had labored in vain, because he—Raphael, the Herald Angel, God's messenger and envoy—had not performed well the work of the Lord, the Lord's message had not been embraced.

All the preparation, all the long hours of rehearsal, all those hymns which had seemed to him so magnificent, all those singers he had believed to be so glorious—all this was for nought. How could he have judged himself sufficient to the task? How could a choirmaster who had never been out of the Beautiful City have convinced himself that he could arouse all mankind to song and worship?

"They did not hear," he said to himself. "They did not understand. They did not welcome the news. I have failed with the most important assignment I have ever had." For the first time, tears of deepest melancholy glistened in an angel's eyes.

Without a word, Raphael signalled the choirs to return to the Beautiful City. Slowly, silently, sadly the singers filed back into the clouds.

Lemuel lingered, offering his hand to help Raphael ascend to Heaven. "Tell me, dear friend," asked the Herald Angel, "what did I do that was wrong? Where did I make my mistake? The people did not hear us, Lemuel. They did not hear."

But the tenor could give no answer.

Still, Raphael knew, the most painful moment was yet to come—for in the Mighty Place his report was awaited. He could not tarry, and he did not.

Within the great hall there was the usual activity: the elders consulting, the scribes busy with their scrolls and pens, the messengers moving rapidly in and out of the hall. Gabriel was there, trumpet ready as always, and Michael, his hand on his sheathed, blazing sword. But as Raphael entered, all activity ceased. All eyes turned as he approached the front of the room, his heart deeply troubled, his eyes downcast.

"Raphael," spoke the Great Voice, "be not troubled. Do not give yourself up to thoughts of failure. I know what is in your heart, and I can see what is in your mind. Know this, you have done well. Even as I commanded, you carried out your task. I am pleased."

The Herald Angel replied: "If, indeed, my task was done according to Thy wishes, please grant me one request."

"What is it, my son?"

41

"Now that my work is finished," Raphael said softly, "I would like to be relieved of my duties as director of the Hallelujah Choir."

Everyone had heard, but no one dared believe his ears. This had never happened before. It would be like Gabriel putting aside his trumpet, or Michael unbuckling his sword.

Then the Great Voice spoke again: "As you wish, Raphael. You may withdraw as director of the Hallelujah Choir. Perhaps a period of meditation would be helpful."

"I am grateful," said the Herald Angel, and turned to leave. But the Great Voice interrupted him.

"Remember this, my son; you were responsible tonight only for the duty you performed faithfully and well."

Raphael hesitated to speak again, but the burden on him was heavy.

"Father," he said, "Thine angel choirs never sang so beautifully as they did this night. Thy universe was never so lovely. No message has ever been more wonderful. But it was as though no one seemed to care. I do not yet know how or where or when I failed, or what I overlooked. For Thy sweet forgiveness I give deep thanks; but within me is the feeling that I have erred. I cannot understand, I cannot understand . . ."

Shaking his head in sorrow, the Herald Angel withdrew. Gabriel spoke to him as he left, and so did Michael, but Raphael only nodded mutely. He returned to his office down the long corridor. There on the desk he made a neat stack of the papers and notes which he had accumulated during the many long months of work and rehearsal. He covered his musical instruments. And then he darkened the room, and left.

In the hall he felt someone brush against him, an angel sweeping swiftly through the corridor. It was the Angel of Death, hurrying toward the great, shining Gates.

One of the nearby messengers explained: "The Angel of Death is going to earth. There has been a slaughter of innocent children."

"Yes, Raphael," added another, "one of the lesser kings seeks to destroy the Gift. But he has been foiled. Mary and Joseph have been warned, and have fled."

The news brought deeper sorrow to the Herald Angel. Had mankind heard God's message, their children would be safe. The Child would be their Prince of Peace. "If only they had heard!" he thought. "If only I had not failed!"

"Raphael!"
"Raphael!"

Had the choirmaster really heard his name called? Or was it only a trick of his imagination? Who could be interrupting his meditations in the Silent Grove? Didn't every angel in Heaven realize that here no one was to be disturbed?

The Herald Angel raised his eyes in astonishment—and found himself peering into the smiling face of Lemuel. The tenor nodded at him pleasantly. "Come, Raphael," Lemuel said as if there were nothing the least bit unusual about his presence. "Come with me."

"Do not disturb me, old friend," answered the choirmaster. "I am thinking."

"And so you have been," Lemuel readily agreed, "for more than nineteen hundred years."

"Years? Centuries? Days? What are they to us? Nineteen hundred years are less than a moment on the eternal calendar," Raphael replied with some annoyance. "If I still feel the need to remain in silence, please observe the rules and allow me to do so. No one else has interrupted me at any time for any reason. You, my closest friend, should know better than to do so!"

The smile left Lemuel's face. "I have been commanded to come here, Raphael. I have been ordered to take you with me."

"Where are we going?"

"To earth."

"To *earth!*" exclaimed Raphael, springing to his feet in alarm. "No, that I cannot do! See here, Lemuel, you know that I have remained here in the Silent Grove since the night we sang for man. I have spoken to no one. I have listened to no one. During all that time, my thoughts have been concerned with just one question— how did I fail in bringing news of the Gift to mankind? What did I do wrong? And only this morning, Lemuel, only this morning did I at last realize the answer!"

Lemuel gazed steadily at his friend, but did not speak.

"Yes," continued Raphael, "today I came to see that the fault was not mine, nor that of the music we sang, nor that of the words of our hymns. The fault lies in man himself! Mankind did not *want* to understand. Men are hopeless."

The choirmaster returned to his seat. Every determined line of his body made it plain that he would not budge. "Yes," he repeated, "men are hopeless. I will have nothing more to do with them."

Lemuel gently placed his hand on Raphael's shoulder. "You have explained why I am here. Our Father knows the path your thoughts have taken. That is why He has commanded me to lead you out of the Silent Grove. Tonight, Raphael, is the anniversary of the journey

48

we made together on the night the Child was born. And tonight we must return."

The Herald Angel knew there could be no further delay. Without even a backward glance, he followed Lemuel out of the Grove, through the streets of the Beautiful City, past the Rainbow Field where the cherubim play, and through the Majestic Gates. Into the darkness the two angels flew.

In that limbo between Heaven and earth, Raphael wanted to linger. There, between star and satellite, there where the past, the present and the future all meet, he wished to tarry. But Lemuel refused.

"We travel far tonight," he said. "There is much for you to see."

"I am ready," Raphael replied. "But before we go further, Lemuel, please tell me one thing. How did it fare with the Child on earth?"

"All but a few men rejected Him," said Lemuel. "After only a short time He was slain."

The Herald Angel covered his face with his hands, and slowly shook his head.

"I will go with you. *Why* we are going I cannot understand—but I will go. I am ready."

Swiftly, soundlessly, the two angels continued their journey until at last they paused to rest on a cloud which hovered just above the flickering lights of a city.

"How high they make their buildings!" said Raphael.

"Some of those buildings reach all the way to Heaven," answered Lemuel. "Mortals call them churches. They have been built to honor God, and to worship His Gift to mankind."

"Impossible!" declared the Herald Angel. "The Son of God was not accepted. You yourself just told me that."

"You have been in the Silent Grove for almost twenty centuries, dear friend. You have much to learn tonight. Come close with me to this building, and read the words that are carved above the door."

Raphael peered at the inscription. *For thine is the kingdom,* he read, *and the power, and the glory, forever.*

"Does this mean," he asked, "that there are still a few men and women on earth who love our Father and His Son as we do?"

"Far more than a few!" answered Lemuel. "Look around you, Raphael—this is a city, one of the biggest that man has ever built. Now look far over, far far beyond that river, to where only a few lights are glimmering in the night. Raphael, both this giant city and that tiny town have many buildings dedicated to the Son of God.

"He was a healer. They have built hospitals in His name on earth, where the sick are housed and cured. He was a teacher. Man has built many places of learning, again in His name and glory.

50

"Look, Raphael, look at the window of this school for children. Do you see all the paintings and pictures the children have pasted to the panes? These are all symbols of the Gift. These snowflakes, these trees, these wreaths, these gaily colored balls—and here, Raphael, here's a drawing of an angel!"

The Herald Angel laughed. It was the first time he had laughed in almost two thousand years. "Why, Lemuel!" he said, "this angel looks like you!"

The tenor snorted. "Please—I'm not quite as plump as that!"

"Oh, this is a wonderful visit!" cried Raphael. "More—please, let us see more."

"We will. Come, let us walk along their streets."

"Oh, no—no, dear friend, we'll frighten them."

"This time they shall not see us. But," the angel added, "look at those crowds! Be sure they do not frighten *you!*"

In an instant the two friends were separated. Raphael found himself being pushed along, pulled, jostled; girls, their faces shining, their arms piled high with multi-colored packages, loomed up before him. Laughing children were under-foot and under-wing. "Merry Christmas," he heard them say as they bumped into one another. "Merry Christmas! Merry Christmas!"

It was too much for the Herald Angel. He darted above the street to the safety of a low-hanging cloud. "Lemuel," he called, "Lemuel, come and get me!"

"I'm right here," his friend answered from the other side of the cloud. "I'll be out as soon as I can straighten my wings."

As Lemuel finally emerged, adjusting his robes and halo, he said: "I was caught in a crowd in front of a toy store. A dangerous place for angels—a toy store on Christmas Eve."

The Herald Angel did not understand.

"You see," the tenor explained, "men and women celebrate the Birth of the Son by exchanging gifts. At this time of the year they remember people they have never even seen, and never will. On this day, as on no other, they find joy in giving. And most of all, Raphael, they give presents to their children.

"But that is not the only way they celebrate the Giving of the

Gift," Lemuel continued. "In their churches they meet to pray by the light of many candles. Look below, Raphael, through the open doors of that little church; you will see how vividly people remember each moment of that night almost two-thousand years ago."

Raphael's face glowed with happiness. "Yes—there is the Mother, the Child, Joseph, and three shepherds. Are they speaking, Lemuel? Or are they singing?"

"You will have your answer, Raphael. Let me take you into one of their homes."

It was a modest home on a starlit street that the two angels selected. As they approached they could see a rainbow of colored lights reflected in the windows; from within they heard voices, young voices.

There were three children in the room, and with them their mother and father.

All were gathered round a large tree that reached to the ceiling, and glowed with small lights and ornaments. Raphael looked questioningly toward Lemuel. "It is a symbol of this holy day," Lemuel replied. "It is called a Christmas tree. And Raphael, don't look so worried. These mortals can neither see nor hear us."

One of the little boys was tugging at his father's arms. "Read us a story before we go to bed," he begged. "Please read us a Christmas story, daddy!"

The husband looked at his wife, and a smile passed between them. "This is the time," the father said, "to read the best Christmas story of all." He walked to the side of the room where a case held many books, and selected a large one from the shelves. The place for reading was already marked.

Slowly, with deep feeling in his voice, he read from the book: "And it came to pass in those days . . ."

The children grew silent as they heard ancient words that were ever new.

"And brought forth her first born son, and wrapt him in swaddling clothes and laid him in a manger . . .

"And there were in the same country shepherds, abiding in the fields, keeping watch over their flocks by night . . ."

Raphael listened and watched, and was carried back twenty centuries. He strained for every word.

"And the angel said unto them: 'Fear not, for, behold I bring you good tidings of great joy which shall be to all people. For unto you is born this day in the city of David a Saviour which is Christ the Lord."

Now the Herald Angel could contain himself no longer. "Your words, Lemuel!" he whispered to his companion. "Those are the very words you sang as you walked through the clouds!"

But before the tenor could reply, new sounds filled the air—laughter, and from the house glad cries of welcome. There in a semi-circle on the snow-covered lawn were children, laughing children, tall and short, thin and chubby, their eyes as bright—yes, Raphael decided—as bright as those of the cherubim.

"They have come to sing Christmas carols," Lemuel explained. "It is the custom."

The children's faces glowed with the twinkling red, green, blue, yellow and white lights of the Christmas tree. The tallest boy stepped forward. He raised his arms high in a signal for quiet; higher, higher—and then he brought them down, and led the group in song.

"Glory to God in the Highest," they sang, "and on earth, peace, good will to men!"

This was the first time in almost twenty centuries that Raphael had listened to a group of singers. With the interest of a professional musician, he observed the way the young voices blended, and watched the confident gestures of the young conductor. "They have a pleasant freshness in their voices," he thought. "They stay on key. I could do much with them."

Then, suddenly, the Herald Angel became aware of the *words* of the carol. They were *his* words! It was the song of the Angel Choir on the night the Child was born!

"Lemuel," he shouted, and tears of joy streamed down his face, "they are singing the song of the Heavenly Chorus. It wasn't lost— our songs were never lost! Our message was heard! They heard us, Lemuel! We did not fail!"

He closed his eyes tight shut. He raised his arms toward Heaven. "Father," the Herald Angel whispered, "Father, I thank Thee!"

And from above—Raphael heard a high note, a low note and a middle note. Three cherub voices, voices bubbling with happiness, picked up the refrain. And then they were joined by others—by the Hallelujah Choir, the Vesper singers, the Jubilee Chorus, the Angelus Choir, and by all the pure sweet voices of all the cherubim.

The magnificent sound rose. Slowly the choirmaster turned, rapture lighting his face—his left side to Heaven, his right side toward the children on the lawn. The voices of the two spheres blended into a joyous carol that resounded through the skies.

And Raphael, the Herald Angel, led the mighty chorus.

— THE END —